Disney

THE MUPPETS

Little, Brown and Company

Hachette Book Group
237 Park Avenue, New York, NY 10017
Visit our website at www.lb-kids.com

Little, Brown and Company is a division of Hachette Book Group, Inc.
The Little, Brown name and logo are trademarks of Hachette Book Group, Inc.

The publisher is not responsible for websites (or their content) that are not owned by the publisher.

First Edition: July 2012

ISBN: 978-0-316-20130-8

10 9 8 7 6 5 4 3 2 1

IM

Printed in China

Book design by Maria Mercado

THE MUPPETS
Kermit's Costume Caper

by Martha T. Ottersley
illustrated by Amy Mebberson

LITTLE, BROWN AND COMPANY
New York   Boston

It's been said that nobody can throw a super-awesome costume contest
like the Muppets, and now it's being said again:
Nobody can throw a super-awesome costume contest like the Muppets.

One of those super-awesome costume contests is happening
tonight, and the PRIZE is going to be super-awesome, too—
ONE HUNDRED GOLD BARS!

"Everyone put your name in this hat," says Kermit. "I'll draw a name to select the judge."

Little does Kermit know that Rizzo is making sure ALL the names in the hat are his!

"Heh heh heh," Rizzo laughs to himself. "When I am the judge, I can pick *myself* as the winner of the costume contest! With a hundred gold bars, I can finally get a cheese-fondue swimming pool!"

Kermit picks a name out of the hat—and it's Rizzo's! The rat will be the judge of the costume contest.

"Okay," says Rizzo, "one by one, show me your costumes. Kermit goes first."

"Guess what I am," Kermit says to his friends.

"Give us a hint," says Fozzie Bear.

"Okay," says Kermit. "I'm a very good listener."

"Hmmm. Are you my grandma?" Fozzie guesses.

"No," says Kermit. "I'm an ear! An EAR OF CORN!"

"Aha!" says Fozzie. "That's *corny*! Good one!"

Next it's Fozzie Bear's turn. "Guess what I am!" he shouts. "I am green, and I am chilly."

"Are you Kermit the ice cube?" Rowlf laughs.

"Close," says Fozzie Bear. "I am COOL AS A CUCUMBER! Wocka! Wocka!" Fozzie realizes his ice is starting to melt. "I am also IN A PICKLE!" he adds. "Can someone please get me a towel?"

Rizzo calls out, "Gonzo and Camilla, it's costume time!"

"Guess what we are!" says Gonzo.

"You're sweet-and-sour chicken to go?" Dr. Teeth guesses.

"Good one!" shouts Gonzo. "But no. We're a TRAFFIC JAM! Beep, beep!"

"Bawk, bawk," agrees Camilla.

"Okay, my turn," says Rowlf. "What am I? Other than kind of embarrassed."

"You're raising the roof?" guesses Fozzie.

"You've got the weight of the world on your shoulders?" Gonzo guesses.

"Those are pretty good guesses." Rowlf chuckles. "But I'm IN THE DOGHOUSE!"

"Oh, Mr. Judgey Rat!" Miss Piggy sings. "I'm ready for you now."

A very special glittery orange curtain opens to reveal...

Dr. Teeth, Janice, and the rest of The Electric Mayhem Band appear, dressed as rocks. They don't wait for their friends to guess.

"We will ROCK YOU!" Dr. Teeth laughs.

"Yeah, but whatever you do, don't take us for *granite*!" Floyd says, nodding.

"This costume, like, totally *rocks*!" adds Janice.

"*ROCK AND ROLL! ROCK AND ROLL!*" Animal shouts as he cartwheels across the floor.

Two Muppet cows stroll by dressed as housekeepers.

"I know what you are!" shouts Fozzie Bear. "MILKMAIDS!"

Then, two monkeys with briefcases go bananas.

"You are, like, totally into MONKEY BUSINESS!" shouts Janice.

And then two dachshunds dressed as dog biscuits go tumbling down the hall.

"There go the ROLLING BONES," cracks Rowlf.

Just then, a large and very strange-looking green thing appears from behind the door.

The Muppets hear the voice of Dr. Bunsen Honeydew saying, "Don't be alarmed. It's just me and Beaker."

Statler and Waldorf watch the Muppets dance in their costumes.

"What are you supposed to be?" asks Statler.

"Same as always," says Waldorf. "BORED TO TEARS! Ha ha! Ho ho! And what are you dressed as?"

"Me?" says Statler. "I'm DOWN FOR THE COUNT."

"Then I'm changing my costume to a COPYCAT!" says Waldorf.

Janice peeks her head out from behind a curtain. "Wait, I have another costume!"

Kermit jumps in, saying, "I don't know, Janice. It might not be fair for you to have two costumes in the contest."

Rizzo declares, "We did not limit the number of costumes. I'll allow it."

"My costume," says Janice, "like, involves opening and closing this flap."

"Ready? Open it."

"Now close it."

"Open it again."

Last but not least, Rizzo the Rat says he has a costume, too, and will also be entering the competition.

"I smell a rat!" cries Miss Piggy. "You're the judge! You can't compete with a costume! That would not be fair at all!"

"Tell it to the judge," says Rizzo. "Oh, wait. Ya just did—and he doesn't care! Now get a load of a *real* winning costume."

Now that the costume show-and-tell is over, the Muppets gather around to see who will be the winner.

"The winner of this year's Muppet costume contest…" Rizzo yells, "is Rizzo the Rat, for the Pie-Rat!"

Rizzo and the other rats are the only ones who clap.

Everyone else boos as Rizzo the Pie-Rat gathers his stolen booty. His claw scratches one of the gold bars as he scrabbles to put them in a pile.

"Hey, wait a minute!" cries Rizzo. "These aren't bars of gold! They're gold-foil-wrapped *chocolate* bars!"

"I can't buy a cheese-fondue pool with chocolate bars," complains Rizzo. "And worse than that, I just started the Ratkins diet! I can't eat chocolate for WEEKS!"

"No problem," says Kermit. "I'll be happy to take that chocolate off your hands and share it with everyone. We'll all be winners!"

"B-but…" Rizzo tries to protest.

"I should have gone as a SOUR GRAPE!"